Two Hearts One Love

Eva Lucas

HEARTSTRINGS PUBLISHING

St. Louis, Missouri

i

To all lovers who have gone before and those who have yet to come.

Contents

Chapter 1: LE INFINITO

A familiar mix of nostalgia and anticipation warms my heart as I return to my childhood home.

My Aunt Linda had lovingly raised me, for my parents were unable to. The bond we share runs deep. I needed to visit and check up on her at least twice a month, mainly because I missed her. Aunt Linda has a way of making me feel understood, accepted, and loved.

As my Uber rolls up, I see a man leaving her house. He is ruggedly handsome and of Mexican decent. His wavy black hair is all over the place, and I am astounded by his remarkable fitness, considering he is in his mid-fifties.

He sees me and flashes me a huge smile as he walks up. "Hi, you must be Hailey. Linda has told me about you, and it's a pleasure to meet you; my name is Ernie."

We chat, and he talks about my aunt and how they met. At this point, my aunt is at the door, excited to see me. "Come in, sweety. I want to hear all about your new job."

With a hug and a kiss, I notice the childhood comforting smells of rosemary and coffee. Whenever I miss home, I put these two scents together, and I feel like I am back in her warm protective shield. Aunty has a way of making me feel understood, accepted, and loved.

"I want to know more about this guy, Ernie. So, he is your carpenter?" My Aunt smiles, and I don't think I have ever seen such a degree of happiness with a visible sense of contentment.

"Yes, I wanted him to fix the damage from the storm, and at first, when he flirted with me, it made me think it was a pattern; maybe he came on to all his female clients. I continued to hire him for other things. Something always needs fixing around here, and I even considered breaking a window to see him again.

He called one day and asked me for a date, and we have been together ever since. I'm happy, Hailey."

"Wow, Aunt Linda! I'm happy for you. How is it that you are getting more action than me? Do I need to go to the Aunt Linda School of Dating?" We laugh our asses off.

She says, "Take your mind off your thoughts and get a facial, join a gym, get your nails done, get a new dress. Something that shows that beautiful skin of yours; everything you wear looks fantastic on you."

"I do get facials, and my current job requires quite a few steps. I already have eight thousand steps today. After my shift tonight, the sky's the limit! I may have twice that. My job is my gym!"

We both chuckle, and Auntie says, "You could also fall for a rich man and not work at all. Every day could be a spa day."

"Rich man?" I give my Aunty a skeptical glance. Yes, a wealthy man would be a bonus, but the real lottery would be someone who would love me for being me, someone who would have my back. When you're in love, you don't care about the low balance in the bank account.

"You care about how he makes you feel, how he looks at you, and the sweet nothings he whispers in your ear. You care about the next exciting adventure together, and every kiss is as passionate as

6

the first. When you are in love, it should inspire a sense of security and trust, allowing you to be vulnerable without fear of judgment."

Auntie need not know these aspects. The way he touches you and ignites a fire in you, a passion you can hardly control, stirring your soul with an undeniable intensity. I think she is getting all of the above with Ernie.

"Love is where my heart is, and it is priceless, but money wouldn't hurt." We both smile; I remind Auntie that my love life has been scarce.

"Hailey, your happiness will come if you let it. I can see true love in your future. Open your heart and mind, and you must see it too."

"You promise?"

Auntie raises her eyebrows and says, "I promise you will find love, honey; how could any man let you slip away? You're a woman with a loving heart, so gifted and loyal.

"So, you see a boyfriend in my future? Aunty, your clairvoyance is appreciated," I laugh. "Who knows what hobbies you have been picking up here by yourself?"

"Ernie keeps me busy, and I'm getting facials."

She grins and blows a kiss, pushing me to get up. "Let's make lunch before it gets late." She makes a beautiful lunch of grilled chicken and roasted vegetables. We catch up about the neighborhood, and she tells me everything there is to know about Ernie.

"I love you Hailey. Take it easy on yourself; everything you want will come to you quickly. You're the most beautiful and talented girl out there, and you should always walk with your head up high."

"I love you, Auntie," I say, hugging her tight.

As I look back at the house one last time, I couldn't help but smile, grateful for the love that had bloomed within those walls.

On the way back to my apartment, the train ride relaxes me. As I see the notable iconic structures of New York City and passing the most famous and romantic landmark, the Empire State Building, I can't help but think about its significant role in love stories. I think about my aunt and the simple life she led. My Aunty radiates a sense of joy and self-assuredness, making single look effortless and enjoyable.

My Family fell apart after my parents let their addictions get the best of them. My sperm donor ran away with a burned-out stripper, and we've never seen him since, which is a blessing.

Although it would have been much better if my mother had run away too, she managed to stick around with her unpredictable behavior, erratic mood swings, neglect, and making me feel responsible for her unhappiness. Life was miserable then, and I was just so young. I was exposed to many things normal children shouldn't be exposed to.

I don't think any child should ever get to see their mother passed out from drugs or witness her having sex in the same room. I was praying to get killed or kidnapped, but that never happened. Instead, my aunt came to rescue me. She was a police officer, so taking me away from my mother was easy, not that my mother cared anyway.

I'm twenty-eight and still trying to overcome the trauma of living with my mother. And the trauma of being in a family house that was never quiet. It was either drug dealers pounding on the door or my parents loudly drinking and partying like they didn't have a child. God knows I suffered and spent a lot of money to get my emotional baggage under control.

Aunt Linda was divorced and alone, and I was so happy to be with her when it was all said and done. My mother didn't fight for me even though it probably cut into her welfare money. We all know where that went. Aunty took care of me, paid for all my therapy sessions, took me to school, supported me all through college, and bought me all the things I needed for college, and I will forever be grateful to her. She had boyfriends come and go, and she never put up with any shit! To say she is my role model would be an understatement. But I want more. I want a soulmate to build a life with someone with the same hopes and dreams.

Maybe I feel this way because I know what love feels like. I've been in love once, and though we were in our late teens, it was a cherished time in my life. Those were the moments in my life that I would love to repeat.

Luca.

The train stops at my station and thankfully clears my mind. I shouldn't go back there. Luca abandoned me, and there is no need to reopen old wounds. Maybe he didn't even feel the same way. Luca was eighteen and I was seventeen. We had an overwhelming desire to be together. It was a powerful connection, and we constantly thought about each other and experienced intense emotional and physical attraction. But if that wasn't love, then why did it feel so good?

*****

"I got it!" I yell out excitedly, popping open a bottle of wine at my roommates' surprised faces when they enter the house.

"I got the job at LE INFINITO!" I yelled again, and this time, I got undivided attention.

"Really?" Beth asked.

"Yes,"

I show them my sexy work outfit and name tag. "Got this today. I'm a bartender at the most iconic bar. LE INFINITO."

The bar is an architectural masterpiece adorned with polished marble countertops and an impressive collection of ornate chandeliers.

Additionally, the bar has a beautiful view of Central Park from the rooftop. According to my coworkers, it was a frequent stop for NYC's rich and famous. The Stones and Billy Joel were regulars when in town.

Connie is more excited than me as she pours the wine. Congrats, baby girl! Does this mean you're going to give your art a rest?" Connie makes an appreciative glance around the room at my exquisite paintings.

"No, I'll continue to paint. It is my true passion. I must step out of my comfort zone to pay the bills, and I know I'll make bank at LE INFINITO slinging drinks. This temporary shift may lead to opportunities. Maybe I'll meet the love of my life.

Connie Laughs. "I can see it now, a hunk of a man walking to the bar. He orders a Bombay tonic and asks, "Can I get your phone number on the side?"

I laugh and add, "I wish it was that simple."

"I know, right," I giggle. "But I won't have to worry about money anymore."

"I heard the boss is a super sexy and handsome dilf or diddo," Beth shrugs.

I pause to think. I know DILF, but DIDDO is new. "What's diddo?"

"You're kidding," Beth says, looking at me like I am suddenly five. "It's Dad I'd Do."

"Well, how old is this dude? Are we talking old or really old? I can't go for one of those saggy old man butts."

We all laugh when Beth reminds us of the episode of "Sex in the City" when Samantha meets the guy with the saggy butt.

I snort. "I don't care how many attributes they have; a saggy butt just won't work!"

After two weeks of working at LE INFINITO, I realize my roommates and friends are not as wrong about the boss as I thought. Throughout the day, my male and female coworkers exchange their collective admiration for the owner/boss. The girls swoon over the thought of him, and the guys try to guess how he is the way he is, coming to ridiculous conclusions that end with how they want to be like him. I haven't seen him yet, but I anticipate the man more than the coming of the sacred advent.

From everything I've heard, I am already attracted to the man. Tall, handsome with green eyes, beards, fit muscles, and Italian. There's just something about an accent on a fine man.

But apart from the talk of the sexy boss, I am having a decent time here and made a few new friends. I have worked as a bartender before, but never in a place this classy. It beats the corner bar back home.

I multitask and deal with a large crowd each night, different personalities of people from all walks of life. I must be on my toes and give service with a smile. The good thing is I earn significant money and meet interesting people.

At the same time, the good goes with the bad. There are always a few assholes in the mix. Some are rude, while others are impatient, along with the occasional sexual harasser. I sure like having a bouncer around.

"Everyone, the boss wants a meeting," Hulio, the manager says, eyes wide and looking like a deer caught in headlights. "He wants to see everybody."

"Everybody?" A woman asks, and he nods in confirmation.

"Come on, one at a time, and you can't keep him waiting," Hulio urges, gesturing and demonstrating with both his hands.

Murmurs fly about, but everyone obeys, entering the big office to see the boss. Rumors and stories start flying about; some say he's looking for a rat in the team, some say someone stole money, and some say he's scouting for someone to replace Hulio.

I'm not scared because I didn't do anything wrong, and I stay composed and pray that I don't lose my voice or stutter like a child.

It finally gets to my turn, and I climb the stairs as calmly as possible. The double doors open as soon as I stand in front of it, and a large and beautiful office comes into view. My jaw drops as I look around, but I try to control my expression because of the man sitting behind a large, wide oak desk at the far end of the room. I can't see his face because he has his head bent down, looking at a file. My heels click on tiles as I walk close to the desk.

"Name and role?" he asks without lifting his head, his deep voice vibrating off the room's walls.

I stop walking. "Hailey Jones, bartender."

"Hm," he sounds with his throat, clicks his pen on the file in front of him, and looks up. The moment our eyes meet is one I won't forget in a hurry. They were right; his eyes were green, a dark, sexy green that can make you feel weak in the knees. I watch as the frown on his face relaxes, and he leans back into his leather chair and looks me over from my head down to my toes. I suddenly start to feel warm and mushy.

"Hailey Jones," he repeats and looks at me again. This time, he took his precious time on each curve and length of my body. I don't think this is the way he looked at everybody.

"Yes, sir."

I am a bit tall, and people always comment on my long, slender legs, so I take the time to keep them toned up. I have curves in the

12

right places and hips that are the perfect size. No Kardashian ass here! I don't have a lot of breasts, just barely going above B, and it haunted me as a teenager, but now I take it in stride, and I'm able to go braless, and the girls are perky.

Today, I'm wearing a bra for our uniforms, which are revealing with minimal coverage. I have confidence in my body and am comfortable in my skin. I have a certain level of modesty as I noticed my boss checking out my long brunette hair that fell over my shoulders in large curls, coinciding with my large brown eyes. I know I'm attractive, but the way the boss looks at me, it seems like the boss is realizing that, too.

He slowly gets up, and my lips part to breathe because of the wonder I see. He is tall and looks more than fit for a man in his fifties. His suit is perfectly tailored, hugging his body in all the right places. His eyes sparkle with a hint of mischief. Check, check, check. All my lists are mentally getting checked. He slowly walks out of his seat and stops when he is right in front of me. His scent is fresh and clean.

"Matheo Ricci," he stretches his hand forward for a shake. "Call me Matheo."

I gulp and put my hand in his. He slowly turns it around and raises my hand to his lips, giving the back of my palm a soft kiss. I almost melted on the spot. "Nice to meet you, Matheo."

His tongue slowly swipes over his bottom lip, and it's so fast I barely catch it. "I didn't know I had such a beautiful employee."

I blush and bite the insides of my cheek. I manage to blubber, "All my co-workers rave about you!"

"What did they say?" he smiles, and even that is sexy with his perfect teeth. "I have horns and blow-out fire?"

"Blue fire, to be precise," I say, and we smile. "No, I'm joking. Everyone speaks great of you."

"I doubt that, but thank you."

He kisses my hand again, and I try not to show how stunned I am. "You're beautiful."

My heart skips a beat, "As are all your employees. Hulio tries his best."

"No, you, Hailey…" he stresses on my name. "…are beautiful."

I look at him, and he does so too. We're in this unspoken eye contest, and I get lost in his beautiful, commanding eyes. There is something about his eyes; they look familiar, but I can't place a finger on it—where have I seen eyes like that? It might be my imagination, but the space between us evaporates slowly, my skin prickles nicely, and I want to sniff him.

Hailey, come back to your senses!

I blink and take a small step backward. "Thank you. Would that be all, sir?"

"Matheo," he corrects.

"Matheo."

He licks his lips again and slowly lets go of my hand. "Yes, that would be all."

He shrugs. "I wanted to put a face on everyone." He leans closer. "You will be hard to forget, Hailey Jones."

As I'm blushing and unsure what to say, I leave him with an awkward, unimpressive, "Alright then. Bye, Matheo."

"See you around, Hailey."

Even the way he calls my name is seductive. I turned around and slowly walked away, knowing his eyes followed my every move. I turn at the door and watch his eyes move from my ass to my face. He looks at me like someone with the intent to unravel me. I've never felt such a sexual pull from someone. I give him a half smile and walk out of the office.

14

My legs finally weakened at the stairs, and I had to hold the wall for support.

Damn.

Chapter 2: Luca

I stare at the list that Margaret from the club gave me, the phone to my ear as she talks. She is supposed to be running this errand, but she has an emergency with her child, and I reluctantly volunteered to help. How on earth did I forget how bad I am at shopping? Especially when it's under pressure.

"If it is not on the list, don't get it. Don't even get a substitute. Hulio would have a tantrum and be a dick," Margaret says, hearing a child screaming in the background.

"Hulio is always a dick," I whine. I didn't sign up for this.

The call ends and Margaret says, "Sorry, thank you so much for this. I owe you one, Hailey," then makes a smooching sound like a kiss, and I sigh. Well, I guess I'm off to the market, my least favorite chore.

Thank God the list isn't long. The bar gets all its supplies from big companies and in large quantities, but occasionally, someone has to rush out to get some things from outside. I still can't complain; it's one of the most straightforward jobs ever.

Before this, I worked part-time as a waitress in college while getting my art degree. And I did portraits of people and pets. I still paint occasionally, but there aren't many clients, and I can't depend on that for survival. I am not worried about money; it will come with trust in the universe's abundance.

I haven't seen much of Matheo, my boss since the day I was in his office. I saw him looking around the club once, and when our eyes met, he didn't look away. I didn't give a shit if my co-workers would see him looking at me that way. Let them start rumors, and nothing has happened.

I have a clear conscience. I don't care. I looked away first because I had to help with a delivery in the back. By the time I came out, he was long gone. My imagination goes wild. I think of the sweet kisses on my hand. I can only imagine those lips touching my body.

Stop it, Hailey

I mean, what is the worst that can happen? He is the boss; he can do whatever he wants.

Is whatever he wants me?

The thought makes me giggle, and the cashier boy gives me a look as he checks out my stuff. I blush embarrassingly and quickly put on my sunglasses. I don't want to be that giggling mad woman. My thoughts are still swooning over Matheo and what exactly he wants, and I leave the supermarket still smiling; the moment I make a turn, though, someone bumps into me, and my bag of lemons fall to the ground, the lemons rolling away.

"Oh shit!" I quickly put down the other bags and ran after the rolling lemons.

"Watch where you're going, lady; you can get hurt," a male voice says, and I'm guessing that's the person that bumped into me.

"Me?" I yell at him. "You watch where you're going. Are you blind?"

The guy pauses to help me with the lemons. "Me? You bumped into me. Maybe you're not seeing clearly with those giant shades in your eyes. The sun is already going down, for Christ's sake."

I stand and glare at him. He's still squatting on the floor, holding the lemon bag.

"For your information, I can see very clearly. It's not your business if I want to wear shades in the evening or morning."

"Wow," he stands up, and I pick up more lemons. And why am I even helping you?"

"Who the hell knows!" I yell and stand up to finally glare at his face. I recognize him instantly, even through my shades. He is way older, but his face still looks the same. The lemons in my hand fall off.

He groans, "Great."

He goes after them and picks them up. "Let me guess, and I am making them fall out of your hand?"

Actually…yes.

I take a step back. It's Luca. Luca from years ago. Luca, my first love. He is taller and way hunkier than the eighteen-year-old boy I knew. I can see his pecs and biceps bulging through the light grey sweatshirt he had on. He is at least six feet three inches, and his dark hair is still in curls on top of his head, but he doesn't have the little bangs he had before. He has light stubble, and his full lips look soft and manly. Then his eyes…

"Excuse me?" He waves his hands in front of me, and I snap out of my thoughts and blink at him. He had a bag full of lemons in his hand. "Your lemons—do I know you?"

I clear my throat and take off my glasses. Luca's eyes narrow and sweep around my face. "I don't know, do you?"

Now, he steps back and breathes out, "Hailey."

Hearing him say my name suddenly makes me feel so angry. He doesn't deserve to call me like that. He doesn't deserve to look at me like he is doing—like he can't believe his eyes. His eyes move from head to toe, and I'm brimming with bittersweet yearnings of years gone by. My heart starts beating faster, and for a second, I think I'm about to have a heart attack. I want to jump up on him and hug him, and at the same time, I want to slap him across the face.

18

No, Hailey, you're over this.

I shake my head and take a step closer. "Give me my bag of lemons."

"Hailey, what—how—?" he stutters, unsure what to say.

I glare at him, but his face takes me off guard again, and I bet I look like I'm squinting. God, he looks so handsome. In my life, I've never seen such a rugged, perfect face. And his eyes, green glow that reminds you of emerald jewels. I remember, in the sun, you can spot gold flecks in them. Hazel green eyes that I'd never forget; it's a blessing and a curse. The eyes—that's why Matheo looked familiar. They both share the same eye color.

Luca has no right to make me feel like this. Not after he abandoned me and disappeared without a trace. I scoff at his face, "What? Can't think of any lies now?"

"What?"

"Give me my bag." I snatch it from his hands. "Wonderful meeting you. Bye."

"Yeah, of course. Run away, isn't that all you ever do?" he says as I walk away.

"Run? I'm not even running yet, Luca. Stay the hell away from me," I say, and hail a taxi.

"I should be saying that to you, Hailey Jones."

It's not until I drive away in the taxi that he remembers my full name. I never knew his full name, and after he disappeared, that was the one thing that haunted me. I didn't know the surname of the most critical person in my life.

As I work, serving customers and cleaning out the drinks display, the day goes on, and I can't stop thinking about Luca. I imagine all the different ways the conversation today would have played out. Maybe if he hadn't bumped into me first, I wouldn't

19

have gone all bazooka on him. But he deserves that. He abandoned me when I needed him most. He promised, and he failed.

A promise is a serious thing to a seventeen-year-old, especially when that's the only good thing in her life. Luca ruined a lot of years for me, a lot of years of detaching and realizing that I was all alone.

"Hailey, stop thinking about him already," I tell myself while making the dirty martini. "You don't need him now. You're better off."

"What?" the lady waiting for her martini asks, thinking I was talking to her.

I smile and extend the drink to her. "Enjoy your time."

She looks at me funny, pays, and leaves. I don't have a say on that, and I deserve the skepticism. Only a crazy person talks to themselves.

*****

A week passes, and just when I begin to not think about Luca and push that experience out of my mind, he shows up in front of me again.

"You know I am already fit, right?" I tell Connie, getting on the treadmill. She dragged me to the gym to exercise, and I know it's all just because of encouragement and getting me out of my funk. "I literally spend all my day on my feet. I get 15,000 steps daily running my ass off at the club!"

"Turn it on already," Connie says with commanding eyes. "I can do this on my own. Both you and Beth keep saying I'm lazy with a fat ass."

"We love your fat ass."

I laugh as I hear someone say, "Hailey?"

I turn, and there Luca is. He has on a baseball cap now, with a black jogger and a blue long-sleeved sweatshirt. The joggers did justice to his long legs, and his arms looked ready to burst out of the shirt. He must have been exercising again because he looked sweaty.

I place a hand on my hip and force my eyes away from his body to his eyes. "Are you following me now?"

His lips twitch in a small smile. "I wish I was. Then I wouldn't have spent the past week looking for you."

I open my mouth to counter, but his words sink in, and I don't know what to say. "What?"

Luca takes a step closer to the treadmill, and I stop myself from taking an action back. The added height from the treadmill made us look almost the same size. Even sweaty, he smells good. "Hailey, we need to talk."

"About what? It's been eleven years," I say, and my voice comes out small like a whisper. Luca is making me feel all types of ways. How can I go from angry to almost melting in less than a minute?

"All the more reason—"

His phone rings, cutting him off. He turns it to mute and looks at me. "I have to go now, but can I get your number? Please?"

That is all I needed to hear because I read my number to him the next second like he was the FBI. Luca smiles says thank you, and I watch him walk away.

"Damn girl, that's some fine man," Connie says, lifting her brows at me.

"Shut up," I blush and turn on the treadmill.

*****

I receive a much more surprising text while waiting for Luca's call or text.

21

"Hello, beautiful Hailey Jones, it's Matheo. Would you care to join me for sightseeing tonight?"

I don't believe the text. When I call and hear Matheo's voice, it is even more sexy. I excitedly agree and start to wonder what the hell I am doing. What am I going to wear?

When Matheo said "sightseeing" he meant art gallery?

A car comes to pick me up. I can't stop smiling and feel like I'm in paradise. I had been too busy for sightseeing adventures, plus no one to go with. Connie and Beth had their lives. I asked Matheo why he had asked me to visit the Metropolitan Museum of Art.

Matheo shrugs. "I got invited and thought you'd like to come along."

I stop and turn to him. "Why pick me?"

He takes a step closer. "Because you're beautiful. Beautiful girls should see beautiful things."

I bite my lip, unable to help how his words make me feel. Matheo takes another step closer, and when I back up, my back hits the wall. We must have been the first to arrive because few people were around. "Matheo…"

His big hands softly land on my waist, and he slowly pulls me closer until my body touches his. His scent is intoxicating, and I almost shut my eyes and drown in it.

He's your boss, Hailey! I gulp. "We shouldn't. You probably have kids my age."

"And so?" he asks. I could feel his breath on my face.

"And so… " I look up at his eyes, which is a bad idea because I can't look away.

Luca has the same eyes.

"I like you, Hailey Jones." He slowly shrugs and leans closer. "And that's all that matters."

Shit, I'm going to kiss my boss!

22

Chapter 3: Matheo

Unfortunately, Matheo and I don't kiss when a group of people passes through. We immediately put some space between us, and Matheo shows me around. I can't believe I thought the "almost kiss" would be the highlight of the evening, but I was wrong. When Matheo starts talking about art in his deep voice, I can listen to him all day. He takes me around to show me his favorite notable artists, and he is quite surprised that I understand every word he says. I even recognize the work of some famous artists he has forgotten.

I shrug shyly under his gaze. "Well, I'm an artist myself."

"Really?"

I nod, grinning from ear to ear. I loved talking about my art; it is one of the only ways to express myself. "Yes, before I got a job at the bar. I was a freelance artist. I still am, but not as much."

"Hm," Matheo says, taking my hand in his and kissing the back of my hand again. "What can't you do?"

I smile, blushing and looking away to hide my face. I'm having a great time, and being with Matheo, known all over town, makes me feel like a diva, maybe even a star. I can't wait to tell my friends about it, and I love how people kept looking at me, wondering who I was and why I was with Matheo.

Then again, he was twenty-five years my senior, and I should be more reserved being seen with a man like him, way older than me. But he didn't even look his age.

Hailey! I mentally scold myself, bringing my head back to reality. I can't go thinking about weird things. Matheo is my boss, but he's so hot!

On the way home, Matheo and I talk more about art, but our minds are elsewhere. I remind him I will see him at work tomorrow, and the sexual tension subsides. He kisses my hand again, reminding me he enjoys my style and company.

When I get home, I tell my friends everything about it, and they are even more excited than I am.

"Wait, he said the words 'I like you'?" Beth asks, a big smile on her face. We are all sitting cross-legged on my bed.

"Yes," I blush furiously. "Then he said that was all that mattered, and we almost kissed. His face was this close to me," I pinch my fingers to demonstrate.

Connie and Beth share an excited look and break into squeals, hitting pillows together.

"Holy shit, Hailey. He's incredibly wealthy and handsome— someone will be wined and dined," Connie says.

"You forgot charming as well," I throw in.

"He must like you then. What are you going to do?" Beth asks.

The smile drops, and I stare at my phone with a pout. "I don't know. He is my boss."

"Wait, it's this about Hot Gym guy?" Connie asks.

Just hearing her talk about Luca gets my heart beating and cheeks tingling. I feel like I am going to cry when I turn to Connie.

"No, but why hasn't he called? It's been a week, and he was the one that suggested we talk. I shouldn't hold on for him; he left me high and dry once before, so he's probably capable of doing it again."

"Hailey, forget about this Luca guy. Obviously, he is playing games. That's what guys our age do. You have a man that likes you; focus on that girl," Beth says.

"But it's Luca," I drawl. Then, I groan and bury my face in a pillow. "What if something happened to him?"

"Don't go thinking that. Didn't you think something happened to Luca years ago, and then he suddenly appeared in front of you eleven years later?" Connie asks, brushing my hair out of my face.

That's true; he could be playing with me all over again.

"So I should completely forget about him?" I ask, and before I can answer, the doorbell rings, and Beth jumps out to get it.

"Hailey, it's for you!" She yells from the living room.

Connie and I both go out, and it's a delivery man. I didn't order anything; I signed after double-checking that it was addressed to me.

We all gather at the coffee table as I tear the package open. It's a big box and inside it is one of the most beautiful dresses I've ever seen.

"Wow," all three of us say, and then I lift the dress. It's so beautiful, and I've seen similar gowns on the body of a celebrity on the red carpet. It's champagne color, thin straps, and covered in sequence. I love it.

"Hailey," Connie calls, grinning as she hands me a small box with a note attached.

I carefully drop the dress and take the box. The note reads—to the beautiful one. Thanks for sightseeing with me.

I gasp and whisper out, "It's from Matheo." I'm too excited and stunned. My voice can't come out correctly. I open the box, and there are two shiny earrings with a tiny stone on them that looks like diamonds. I gasp again and have to sit down so I don't fall.

Connie and Beth yell, fawning over the earrings.

"Still have your doubts about this man?" Beth asks, unable to stop smiling.

I smile. Okay, maybe I can give Matheo a chance. He's intentional and doesn't make me second-guess his feelings. I don't even know what Luca wants to talk about, and I don't even know if he likes me. I'm almost sure about Matheo.

*****

It's my off day, and I have many plans for what I must do. Maybe I will book the facials my aunt was talking about. I think about what Aunt Linda will say when I tell her about Matheo if I actually tell her. The thought makes me giggle. She will definitely freak out and bombard me with a lot of questions. But the ultimate one would probably be, "Are you happy?"

Am I?

My phone rings, and it's an unknown number. I'm tempted to let it ring, but it could be work or something else essential, so I pick it up. "Hello?"

"Hailey?"

A male voice calls out softly. I gasp and almost throw my phone away in surprise. I know that voice.

"Yeah?" I cautiously ask after taking a moment to recoup.

"Hailey, it's Luca," he says, and I can guess he is smiling from his voice.

"Oh yeah, Luca," I gulp, my face flush with embarrassment.

"Is this a bad time?"

I look around my apartment and my half-painted toenails. "No."

"So," he pauses a bit, and I can imagine him shifting from foot to foot if he is standing. "Can I ask you to dinner?"

I bite my lips as my heart does a backflip, "Yes, you can."

26

Chapter 4: The Date

For my date with Luca, I am opting for a maxi dress that shows my neckline and shoes to match. I curl my hair in large, bouncy curls and apply enough makeup to make it look effortless. I don't know why I'm so nervous. It's just Luca, and I've bumped into him twice already. I don't need to be this excited because he finally called and asked me for a date.

I take a taxi, and Luca is classic, standing outside the fancy restaurant when I arrive. He looks up when the cab stops and watches me come out, hands in his pockets.

"Why are you outside?" I ask, seeing him; the question is to distract myself from how good he looks. He wore a beige fitted sweater with black dress pants and dress shoes. His hair is shiny and looks soft and curly. His face looks perfect, green eyes looking at me like he wants to see inside my soul.

Luca removes his hands from his pocket and walks closer. His alluring scent hits me, and I unconsciously close my eyes to take it all in for a few seconds. "I didn't want to miss any of this." He slants his neck—even that looks seductive—and slowly looks me over, head to toe. "You look beautiful. More beautiful than I imagined."

My lips twitch in a smile, "You imagined?"

He smiles and gestures to himself. "I had to. I didn't want to come underdressed and have people wondering what a beautiful girl like you is doing with a guy like me. Although nothing I could have done or can do would ever compare to how you look."

I blush, "Did someone pay you to flatter me?"

Luca laughs. His laugh is so rich and hearty, and the butterflies in my tummy go crazy on hearing it. His laughter didn't change; watching him laugh, I saw the eighteen-year-old Luca who loved me. Or at least he said he did. "I assure you I'm not flattering you, and it's the truth."

I slowly nod. "You look good yourself." Then I glance around, "and we should go inside. I'm famished."

Starving for his attention.

"After you."

Luca is such a perfect gentleman. There is no trace of the guy yelling at my face the other day, although I prompted most of that, and even then, he was kind and helped me pick up my lemons.

The restaurant has a carefully curated décor and inviting ambiance. Additionally, the food is from farm to table and prepared with meticulous detail.

Luca tells me the restaurant's story and the famous chef who is sure to make this a memorable culinary experience. I trust him, and he orders something for us both: the delicious Caprese salad with bruschetta and seabass with wilted spinach.

We share small chit-chat, mainly about the food and where we both work. I tell him I am part of a team that manages a bar, and he tells me he owns a startup company. He was traveling around and came back to New York about a month ago. He never asks about the name of the club I work in. I'm assuming he knows.

Dinner ends faster than I wanted, and I am already sad about parting ways and not talking about everything I want to. When Luca asks if we can take a walk, I wholeheartedly agree. There is still so much I want to know. The sun is already setting, but as usual, the city is alive and buzzing with people.

"The food was nice, thank you," I say. I offer to split the check, but Luca politely declines.

"Thank you for coming, and I'm sorry about the other day," he mentions. "It's no excuse, but I was having a bad day."

"Me too, I shouldn't have snapped at you."

We stay silent for a moment, and then he sighs, "I've missed you a lot, Hailey."

"Really? Because I have been looking for a long time. You were nowhere to be found; you disappeared without a trace," I pause, looking up at the orange sky, "You promised, Luca."

I met Luca when I was fifteen years old. He had come to play basketball on the court down our street, and I always hung out there after school because my parents weren't back home yet, or they were back but had visitors over, or I was avoiding them—one thing or the other.

That day, I arrived there so hungry and sleepy. I left home angry that morning and hadn't eaten anything at all. Curled on the bench, I fell asleep with my head over someone's duffle bag.

When I woke up, Luca was sitting on the ground beside me, looking at me. I screamed, and he screamed; it was like a scene out of a movie. I was sleeping with my head on his bag, and he didn't want to wake me up. His driver was waiting on him already, and we didn't even get to exchange names. I apologized. He took his bag and ran to a black Mercedes waiting for him. I couldn't stop thinking about the weird boy that waited for me to wake up.

The next day, he came again; I wasn't asleep this time. I watched him play, following his every move with my eyes, smiling when he won and wincing when he fell. He must have noticed and purposely threw the ball to my side, then came to get it. He smiled at me as he picked up the ball, and that was the first time my heart beat wildly because of a boy.

Luca came to sit by me after his match ended, and we exchanged names and talked, getting to know each other. He was older by just one year, and he was coming to play here, all the way from his house, because our school's basketball team was the best, and his coach recommended he play with the guys and challenge himself.

He lived uptown at the fancier and bigger houses and went to a private school. Our lives were so different, but somehow, we became friends and were inseparable.

He started coming to the court more frequently. I excitedly ran there to meet up with him. Sometimes, he bribed his driver to drive us around, and those were the best times ever.

I knew about his father and mother fighting all the time, and he knew about my parents' waste of money and alcoholism. We comforted each other. Even after his required time at the court, Luca kept coming. I sneaked him into my house sometimes when my parents weren't home, and once or twice, I took a bus to his private school and waited for him to leave so we could go somewhere.

We started dating when I was sixteen years old, and it was evident to anyone around that we loved each other and couldn't stay away. Luca had a car then, and he always came around. He even started teaching me how to drive, and we made plans for the future together. I had never met his parents; we were waiting till the right moment. Luca feared his dad would split us up because of my family's background. So mum was the word.

He would attend Boston College to study business and manage his mother's company when he finished. I thought he would go pro with basketball since he was so good, but he wasn't interested in it and only played it because his father wanted him to.

Luca didn't get along with his father, and there were always rumors about his father cheating on his mother. Sometimes, Luca slept over at my place when he couldn't stand his house anymore, he would sneak out early while my parents were out of it, and sometimes we both slept in his car.

During the period when my parents lost everything we owned, I had no idea we'd have to leave the house, but Luca and I met one last time, and he promised he'd always be around no matter what happened. He was about to graduate high school and said that would give him enough leverage to see me wherever I was. We promised to always be there for each other.

"I love you, Hailey," Luca had said, touching my face as we sat cuddled under a tree, "now and always."

"Even when you go to college and my parents decide to sell my kidney for money?" I asked, slipping the joke in there. It wasn't a joke, though. I thought they were capable of that.

Luca laughed his boyish laughter. "Yes, even then. I don't think any girl is as pretty as you in college."

"What if there are?"

"Then I'd tattoo 'Hailey's Boyfriend' on my head," he joked.

I laughed, placing my head over his heart. "You won't, but I love you for saying that."

We were evicted from the house the next day and had to move. I came to the basketball court for weeks, but Luca was nowhere to be found. I called him over and over, but the number was disconnected.

I waited for months, and my mom moved between towns after my father ran away. I cried, thinking that I would never see Luca again. I cried, wondering what I did wrong for him to disappear. I cried, wondering if my family situation suddenly became too much. I cried with the thought that he found someone else better than me and left me for her. I didn't even want to hear the word love or think about it.

Things gradually got better after my aunt took me in. It took a lot of time, but I let the memories go, and I eventually got over him and moved on.

I always try not to think about that time of my life, and now I feel teary, but there's no way I'd cry in front of Luca.

"I didn't abandon you, Hailey; I thought you abandoned me. I thought you couldn't stand not having me around, and you moved on," Luca says, and when I look into his eyes, they look so sincere.

I scoff, "Now, what on earth made you think that? You didn't show up."

"Yes, because my dad sent me away. We had a big fight when I got home. I said things I shouldn't have, and he shipped me to military school. I had no say in it; my age or opinion didn't matter with him pulling strings. It was like a prison," he ran his hands through his hair, "but I sent letters to you. Hundreds of them, and I got no response. I sent them to your house, I sent them to the school, I even sent some to the church."

"What?" I can't believe it. My heart is pounding painfully, and my ears are ringing. Luca didn't abandon me?

"Yes, Hailey. You have no idea how hard that time was for me. I thought about you every day, and I missed you like hell. After I got out, I went looking for you. I found an Asian couple living there, and they said they had been there for five years. I figured you guys stayed until then; if that was the case, you got my letters. I had no idea."

"Luca…" I stop walking and look at him. Tears well up in my eyes as I imagine him looking for me.

"Hey." Luca closes the distance between us, staring at my face. "It's all in the past now. Just one big misunderstanding."

I don't know when, but my hand reaches up and I touch his face. Luca shivers at my touch, closing his eyes for a second and opening them back. They look brighter and dilated. "Are you okay? A military school must have been hard."

He smiles. "It was, but I'm fine now. What about you? Did your aunt treat you better?"

I smile now. "Yes, a Godsend, the best aunt ever."

We start walking again, this time closer than before; our hands are touching.

"And do you happen to have a boyfriend?" Luca asks. When I look at him, his eyes are on his shoes, and his ears are red.

I blush. "No. Do you? Have a girlfriend?"

He shakes his head. "No," pauses, then adds, "and for the record, I was right. I never met any girl as beautiful as you. I don't think any exist."

It feels like time freezes; all I can hear is my heartbeat and warm face.

I don't think I'm over Luca; I don't think I ever was.

He takes me home and leaves me with a kiss and a goodnight, leaving me longing for another taste of passion.

Chapter 5: The Rendezvous

I come to the club early because staying home isn't helping me. My thoughts keep bouncing all over the place, and I can't help focusing on the happy feelings from my date with Luca. I am distracted, and instead of helping around, I mess things up and slow everyone down.

Hulio sees what's happening and gives me the key to the rooftop, asking me to clear my head on the roof. "There is plenty of fresh air up there, and you seem like you can use a break," he says, edging me to go.

Thankfully, I quickly leave before he changes his mind. The rooftop is beautiful. There were plants here that made it look like a garden, but a large part was open with couches and lounge chairs.

The plan is to sit on a lounge chair and take in the fresh air, but that's until I see cans of spray paint. I have no idea who left them on here, but there are many of them, and they aren't empty. My eyes light up, and I decide to distract myself from my Luca problem. I shouldn't be feeling this way after finding each other after all this time. So I paint.

I lose track of time and don't know how many hours pass, but I'm startled and returned to reality when a deep voice calls my name.

"Hailey?"

I turn around to see who it is, half expecting it to be Hulio and half expecting to see a ghost, but neither happens, and I come face-to-face with Matheo. My lips part, but no words come out.

Matheo smiles at me and walks from behind me to the front, eyes on my mural on the ground. "What are you doing?"

"Oh my God," I let go of the paint, and it clatters loudly on the floor as I get up. "I'm so sorry. I saw the paint, and I got carried away. Please don't sue me. I can paint over it. I'm not a vandal."

Matheo chuckles, "Calm down, Hailey." He looks down again. "Is this a bird?"

I look down at it; it is a colorful and majestic bird with open wings. I slowly nod. "It is. It's the bird of happiness. I tend to draw birds when I'm confused or conflicted."

Matheo looks up at me with concerned eyes. "What's going on?"

I can't tell Matheo what's going on even if I want to. It's Luca, and somehow it's tied to him too. I have feelings I shouldn't have for Luca, and he is in the picture, making it all the more confusing.

Matheo takes three steps, and he's right in front of me. His finger tilts my chin up until I am looking at him. "Tell me."

I smile and shrug. "There's nothing to tell. It's just a normal girl's problem. I'll get over it."

"Well," Matheo scrunches his lips as he looks around. "Can I pay for this art? And the one you'd do at my house?"

Now I raise my brows, "What?"

"This is beautiful, and I'd like to pay for it. I'd also like one of these in my house." He walks closer again, and his hand finds my waist. "Come paint for me, Hailey; that should help you distract yourself more, right? And now you can't say no because it's your job, right? You're a freelance artist."

I stare at him dumbfounded and don't know what to do as I give him a confusing nod. Matheo convinces me, and we leave the club without anyone seeing. We get into his Mercedes, and he excuses his driver and drives to his house. I sit in the front seat, my hand out the window, taking in the day's cool breeze and trying to convince myself that I wasn't doing anything wrong going to my boss's house. It's work, and he invited me, and I'm not committed to anyone.

*****

Luca.

I shake the thought of Luca out of my head. We just met. Matheo likes me, and I feel something for him. If he wants to help me distract myself, then I'd let him.

Matheo lives in a penthouse at the top of a twelve-story building. His house takes up all the top floor, and the elevator opens to his living room. It's massive, it's grand and it's beautiful. My jaw drops as I take in the spacious layout while admiring the details of luxury and lavish comfort.

"You like it?" Matheo asks, looking at me with amusement written all over his face.

"Like?" I clap my hands together. "I love it!"

He breaks into a chuckle. "Well, make yourself at home, Hailey."

How does one make themselves at home in such a luxurious apartment? Matheo must like painting because he bought many of them from well-known artists. He brings me a canvas and a paint set that he has lying around. He tells me that he has tried almost everything there is to try. If it spikes his interest, he does it.

And so he had tried painting before and music and even fish farming. I am more than intrigued, and I can listen to him talk for the whole day, and it will be like time isn't passing. He has had his fair share of exciting adventures, and I want to hear about it all.

I get completely engrossed in painting. I decide to paint his big and lavish dining area, complete with a round table and four chairs. I'm so into it that I don't see Matheo leave and return shirtless with two wine glasses. It's not until he dips his fingers into yellow paint and rubs it on my cheek that I startle and turn to him. I gasped inside, seeing him there shirtless before me and looking like a Greek statue with a perfect body.

"Matheo," I breathe out, unable to keep my eyes on his face.

He smiles and extends the wine glass to me. "Care for a break?"

I nod, drop my paintbrush, and take the glass from him. "Down it in a gulp or two?"

He laughs, "On three?"

He counts, and then he gulps down his glass. Matheo has his eyes closed, taking in the wine, and I quickly dip my hand in red paint and touch his pecs.

"Ha!" I call, laughing as I see his startled face.

Matheo laughs, grabbing the paint palette. "You're dead."

I squeal and run off, and he chases me. He gets me quickly with his long legs and tickles me, making me yell and giggle uncontrollably. Then he pauses, pushes my hair out of my face, and his hand pulls my waist closer until my body touches his. I freeze, and my eyes find his green eyes.

Matheo's thumb reaches out and gently caresses my bottom lip. I close my eyes, taking in the electrifying feeling. When my eyes open, they find Matheo's eyes on me, looking darker, and then, in what seems like a split second, he leans down and takes my lips in his.

My eyes shut automatically, and I almost moan into his mouth as he kisses me, one hand around my waist and the other touching my face and holding me in place. I've never kissed a man with so much dominance and assurance. I feel safe that he won't let me fall, and that he would always be there to catch me. That's what the kiss feel like—warm, safe, and perfect. My legs go weak, and Matheo must sense it because he smiles into the kiss and softly pulls away.

37

Then, my feet leave the ground in a second as he picks me up, bridal style.

I have no words and want to keep kissing him as my arms wrap around his neck. Matheo brings us into a room with a jacuzzi already on. He slowly drops me back on the floor and helps me take off my shirt, and then we both get naked except for my panties and his boxers.

His naked body was wow.

Matheo pulls me in, so I sit above him, and his hands find my hair with a gentle pull, and our lips find themselves again. We kiss, tongues dancing, and breaths coming together as one. I become evident of the hard-on I can feel right under my ass through my lacy panties, but it feels so good I don't want to stop.

Matheo breaks from the kiss, his lips moving to my neck and his hands groping my ass. My head rolls back in pleasure, and I want to let go and forget everything.

Then I heard my phone ring. It's so loud, I wonder how I haven't gone deaf.

"My phone," I whisper out breathlessly.

"Leave it."

I leave it, but the moment it rings again, I return to the reality that I shouldn't be doing this with my boss.

"My phone, I have to get it, Matheo."

I push myself out of the jacuzzi. "It could be an emergency."

Then I grab my clothes and walk out before I hear his protests.

It's Connie calling, and when I pick up, she's crying, and I can hear screaming in the background. Shit. "Connie?! Connie, what's wrong?"

Chapter 6: Desire

I haven't seen much of Matheo since I ran out of his house the other day. He understood my voice's urgency and wanted to drive me home, but I declined and hurried off.

Connie's ex-boyfriend Henry was at it again, drunk and banging at the door. Connie called the cops on him but was still scared he would get through the door. I arrive just in time to threaten him, and minutes after police sirens fill the air, he takes off. Henry is always pathetic and terrified of everyone but tries to act tough by bullying Connie.

She first met him on a dating site; he was charming and fun. The horror came out as soon as she fell for him; the gaslighting, blame, and lying followed. Connie and I went to the station to file for a restraining order after she yelled, "Enough is enough!"

As we go to bed that night, Connie tells me she can't believe she fell for such an asshole. I reassure her we all have been there. I tell her I was with Matheo, and she nearly goes crazy with guilt. I do not feel bad, though. I don't think I was ready for that encounter to happen. I still can't wrap my head around that my boss likes me and is old enough to be my father.

Matheo calls that night to ensure everything is okay and sends a picture of him hanging the dining room painting I did for him. That alone gives me a slight tingle all over. I sleep that night with worry for Connie and a glimmer of joy.

*****

I arrive at work the following morning, unsure of how to feel about me and Matheo's rendezvous the previous day. I was preparing to be out of his sight if it came to that.

I find it hard to understand my feelings when he is near. Caution is the name of the game, or everyone in that bar, sooner than later, will think that I am sleeping with the boss.

The thought of that crossing my mind causes me to shiver.

I can't deny the slight hint of excitement that comes with it, as forbidden love was a trope I never thought I would explore but knew better.

The thought of murmurs going around that I slept with my boss to get my job or to get to the top causes an unsettling stir in my stomach. It is starting to get noticeable.

If anything, it will be outside the bar's walls, with the most extreme caution.

Until then, I reiterate my stance to keep us out of compromising positions. And I mean that in the literal sense.

"Is something wrong?" Hulio's voice calls out, startling me.

I shake my head nervously. I wonder how long I stood there, lost in thoughts.

Hulio nudges me to return to work, and a notification pings on my phone.

Shit.

I turn around to ensure that Hulio didn't hear the ringer and immediately shut it off.

I've been so disconnected from reality that I forgot to drop my belongings in the locker room. Phones aren't allowed during work hours to keep us from these distractions.

I take a glance at my screen before attempting to put it away.

Wait!

My hand snaps back up instantly.

It was Luca who called.

My cheeks flush red, and I glance over my shoulder to ensure no one is watching me. Slowly, I creep into a corner of the bar and swipe open the notification.

To the most beautiful woman in the world,

Would you do me the honor of having dinner with me?

Location: My home

Time: I'll meet you at 42nd and Broadway at 7:00. We will cab it and walk part of the way so you can see the neighborhood.

P.S. I may or may not be considering opening a restaurant soon, so [somebody] would value your opinion.

I chuckle.

I respond with an excited "yes" and the cutest emojis before teasing him that I am yet to accept.

Should I tell him where I work?

I sigh and place the phone over my beating heart, then I look up, and my eyes catch Matheo's large, blurred portrait at the bar. It's blurred out on purpose so no one sees his face clearly, but I can outline his back and jawline, and that's him.

I realize that I hadn't seen him all morning, unlike him. I didn't mind, though, as I need space to think about what I want, what I am doing and going to do.

He is a man whose age has already knocked on the doors of fifty. I know they say age is but a number, but I am not sure of what I'm doing. Plus, before he liked me, I saw the number of mystery women that flocked around him. Those are not people I want to compete with or have issues with.

Maybe I'll get more perspective when I visit Luca's house today.

I shrug my shoulders and tuck my phone away when another notification from Luca comes in. I bite my lips and smile at the subtle sexiness of the text. I stop responding so I don't spend the entire workday glued to my phone.

As though on cue, Hulio's voice calling me out, resounds from the other end of the bar.

Luckily, the bathroom was opposite, so my excuse was handy.

Alas, all it took was a few words of reprimand for me to get my head in the game. Nevertheless, I couldn't wait to get off my shift.

After a quick change of clothes, I ran out of the club and took a taxi to the corner of 42nd and Broadway. As I leave the cab, Luca stands on the corner, looking immaculate as always. His hands were in his pocket, swaying back and forth in his casual fitness— Blue Jean pants, a black top that hugs his body, and a simple scarf around his neck. I've never seen a guy wear a woolen scarf so well. And what a gentleman, insisting on paying for my cab.

I remember never having mentioned the name of the place I work, so I made a mental note to do that in case of next time.

Look at you, pathetic!

I was thinking of the next time already.

"Luca," I call, and when he looks up, "So good to see you."

He smiles and gives me a friendly hug. "Hi, Hailey." I already feel as though I'm melting inside.

The butterflies in my tummy return tenfold, and I blush, smiling at him. "Hi you, Mr. Persistent."

He chuckles, "I've always wanted to walk a girl home, and this time, it's even more perfect since it's my house, although we will have to take a cab to get close unless you want to walk five miles.

"Oh really?" I ask, and I feel like my cheeks will burst into flames.

He nods, and I do, too.

"Well, I am happy that I can help you get something crossed off your bucket list."

My hand reaches up, and my fingers lightly stroke his scarf. It's so soft. "This looks so good on you."

He looks down as if he's becoming aware that the scarf is still on him. Then he starts undoing it.

"I brought it for you." He puts it over my neck and gently ties it. "I figured you'd be underdressed. It's a bit chilly."

I can't stop smiling as I touch the scarf on my neck. Luca is so thoughtful, and it even smells like him. "I'm not even going to protest because I love it."

"Shall we?" He gives me his hand, and I put mine in his. It fits perfectly, and we start walking hand in hand, as we hail a cab.

I can't even believe it, and I keep staring at our hands together to ensure I'm not dreaming. It's happening. Luca is holding my hand as we walk. It's bold, it's romantic, it's comforting and safe.

"About the restaurant, were you serious?" I immediately clear my throat to keep myself from swooning further.

"What?"

"The restaurant you mentioned in the invite?"

"Oh? Well, would you like that?" I hear Luca tease in a husky and low tone.

"What," I ask, a bit confused.

He is delighted at my confusion, and I hit his chest and ask him to be serious.

"This may seem like I'm jumping to conclusions, but I still like you, Hailey. Enough to want every form of commitment with you—"

The honk of the cab Luca orders distracts him from finishing his confession because, with the way he stopped abruptly, hovered over me, and stared into my eyes as he began, there was much more to be said.

Not until the metallic taste of blood hit my tastebuds did I realize I had been biting the insides of my mouth.

I'm not too fond of my mind trying to race faster than I can keep up. Too many questions and uncertainties hit me all at once. Paranoia is building within me.

Suddenly, Luca gently squeezes my hand, giving me that extra layer of tenderness and intimacy.

I don't know if he sensed my unease, but he did the most reassuring thing.

I want to ask him to continue what he started earlier, but that is probably not the line of conversation I want to hear. The silence isn't helping matters either.

I shift uneasily, and he squeezes again like it's the most normal thing ever, and he is used to it before he strikes up a conversation.

Luca talks to me about his work and how he lives alone because his last roommate and guy best friend nearly made him go crazy. He loves him still but can't share a house with him anymore.

I am intrigued, and we go on and on exchanging experiences.

I tell him about my lovely roommates Connie and Beth and how I met Connie at the university, and Beth was her childhood friend she reunited with again while house hunting. They could be a handful, but we make it work, and I love them.

The cab drops us near Cobble Hill in Brooklyn. The historic brownstone houses with tree-lined streets had a sense of community offering a peaceful atmosphere with many local parks and small shops that added to its unique character. Cobble Hill provides perfect balance of residential tranquility and easy access to the bustling city life of New York City.

In no time, we arrive at Luca's house, and it is beautiful. Necessary to add, homely. That is unlike many bachelors. Their homes are usually plain vanilla, with no personal touch to them.

It's not any grand penthouse, but it is undoubtedly a costly home.

He owns a golden retriever, too, named Quick. I laughed after hearing the name. Quick. He looked like he loved me instantly with his well-manicured and beautiful brown fur.

The house is even more perfect with its open floor plan and high ceilings. All the furniture looked special ordered, a leather couch that I could see the two of us snuggling to watch our favorite Netflix. A flat-screen, complete with gaming equipment and a kitchen any chef would die for.

Luca tells me the house has three bedrooms, and I don't even know it's possible to fall in love with a home until now. He asks me if I would be interested in a tour, and I agree even before I can think about the privacy I was about to intrude.

I can already imagine two kids running around here with Quick.

Hailey! I scold myself for thinking that, but my cheeks get hot.

"Hailey," Luca calls, and he's standing before me. He comes closer and reaches for my hands, squeezing them in his. "I just want you to know I don't do this with girls."

I smile, "Oh really?"

"Yes," Luca looks so sincere I start believing it's not his regular pickup line.

I appreciate that he is trying hard to be as vulnerable as possible with me. Most men these days don't show their emotions.

"Okay."

"I haven't invited any girl over or prepared to cook a meal for her. I'm doing this because it's you," Luca says, and my heart feels like it will skyrocket out of my chest.

"Seeing you again at the gym, it was like we didn't lose any years between us. I know we did, and you're a much more beautiful, mature, and talented woman right now, and it's all fascinating to me. I want to get to know this version of you and start up something with you if you want it as well," he pauses, and all I can do is look at him.

I look at his sexy green eyes; all I see is sincerity.

Luca gives me a small smile. "It can be a bit overwhelming, and I'm shaking right now," I stutter, and we chuckle.

"Take your time. You can give me an answer whenever you're ready. I'd be here waiting."

I don't get to say anything or want to when he pulls me closer for a hug.

The electricity that shoots through my entire body leaves my legs faltering under me.

Luca notices this and holds me tighter against his chest. I hadn't seen the swift movement of his muscles coming. I giggle slightly against his chest as I stabilize myself, and when I look up, I can see the hunger in Luca's eyes.

He stares down at me, his pupils darken, and all the moisture in my throat disappears.

We remain like that, insatiable desire filling the air, our breaths becoming heavier until Luca finally pulls away.

"I think I should feed you first," his raspy voice erupts in a low growl before he turns away.

My thighs are clenched in place, calming the excessive throbbing going on down there.

The temperature in the room rises, making me hotter and hotter.

"I think we can get to that later," I groan and plunge forward to the counter, turning him to face me.

In an instant, Luca turns around, devouring my lips with his. It is rough, filled with hunger and overwhelming desire, but perfect.

I moan severally into his mouth, enjoying how our tongues fight for dominance.

My hands find their way underneath his shirt, tugging it off, dying to feel the warmth of his skin on mine.

He senses my agitation and frantic need to take it off, so he chuckles lightly against my lips before creating a gap between us to put me out of my distress.

I run my fingers up and down his back, my fingernail threatening to dig into his skin and claw some flesh out.

His kisses are swifter and hungrier, and his hands move from roaming all over my clothes to sneaking beneath them.

His finger grazes my left nipple, and I let out a muffled moan before inching closer to his body.

He cups my b-cup bra nicely, admiring the lacey material that adorned my cleavage.

I move back to take off my clothes as the sex-starved, impatient Hailey that I was.

I'll regret calling myself this by morning, but till then.

I use those mini seconds to catch my breath because we are back hovering over each other in no time.

"Are you sure you want to do this?" he pulls back, leaving us panting and hungrier for more.

Is he crazy?

Am I sure I want him to fuck me till I forget how to spell my name? Or what? Is taking off my clothes acting to him?

I appreciate his gentlemanliness, but now is not the time.

Please, Luca!

I send him a death stare, and he immediately comports himself by pulling me closer. His hands find their way to my ass cheeks

47

immediately, and he massages them intently while his mouth places wet kisses from the side of my neck, over my jawline, and down my chest, and they linger around my bra.

He uses his tongue to draw circles around my hard rock nipples, nibbling one after the other, making the see-through lace soak up.

My head is thrown back, my lips parted and making way for unsteady breaths while my hands go behind his neck, nudging him to do more wicked things to me.

"Fuck it, Luca," I whimper suddenly.

I pull back and yank off my bra. And he smirks.

This asshole was teasing me on purpose.

I watch his eyes travel hungrily around my body, his slightly visible Adam's apple move up and down, and his pupils are hardly visible when his gaze returns to mine.

Luckily, he doesn't waste time to claim back my lips. He picks me up instantly, wrapping my legs around his torso as he walks back towards the counter to place me atop.

Luca steals his lips from mine and trails the length of my body with them instead. His hand grabs my neck, pushing my upper body back and following down my thighs.

Involuntary, my legs spread wider, giving him easier access. I use my elbows to support my body, allowing him to do whatever he wanted.

I was eager. I was ready.

Luca stands back up and claims my lips briefly before turning to what he cares more about: my nipples.

He uses his tongue to flick my nipples wickedly, and I cry ecstatically.

His hands work on my other nipple before trailing down to my inner thighs, where he finally feels the moisture level.

"Someone's having a waterfall somewhere."

I roll my eyes at the break in transmission.

He returns to work, using a finger to shift to pull my panties off. Then, using his magic finger, he strokes my clitoris repeatedly, causing me to lose balance on my elbows and scream his name.

He doesn't stop.

Not like I want him to, anyway.

In a flash second, one that I do not recall, a finger finds its way inside me.

I whimper.

Slowly, he picks up the pace with his fingers while I cry out in euphoria. Another finger joins the party while his mouth swallows my moans.

Finally, I wail out.

"Fuck me, Luca," I plead.

He nods but doesn't immediately obey. He swaps the activities going on as he replaces his fingers with his mouth and addresses the upper part of my body with his fingers.

Luca devours me like he had waited for this moment all his life.

Frankly, that was how I feel, so I equate it. It doesn't take long until I have the best orgasm of my life. And I am pretty sure there is more in store for me.

Moments later and his hard cock lingers at my entrance, teasing me till I can't wait any more.

"Please."

"Please, what?"

"Please, fuck me."

"Who?"

He is enjoying himself watching me miserable. My pride can't kick in at this point.

I want him desperately.

"Please fuck me, Luca."

In a matter of seconds, he is inside me. He picks up his pace slowly until my body adjusts to his entrance.

With each thrust, our moans and groans filled the air, the tempo increasing as our breaths in synchrony.

These moments are beyond what words can ever perfectly describe.

He holds my body tight against his and rams his entire length into me at a heightened pace.

I scream to him more than I can count, my toes curl so hard. I am confident my knuckles are turning white, but I couldn't care less.

His body stiffens against mine, and I know we are reaching climax at the same time.

Finally, only our raggedy breaths fill the air.

We remain transfixed, my hand around his neck, our bodies in place as we try to steady our breathing.

I get down from the counter, and my knees fumble.

Damn, I think, and my cheeks flush with embarrassment.

A smile of satisfaction spreads across my face, and I bite my lip.

I push Luca to the sofa, and he smirks at me, "What are you doing?"

"Can you just quit speaking?"

"Sorry, ma'am."

I kneel and stroke Lucas' cock till it attains its full length again. I glance at him and see him watch me with full attention and intent.

He looks ready to take over, but I will not let him.

His lips part slowly as my hands move swifter, up his length and tighter at his cap. A low groan escapes the back of his throat, and I pull my hands back, causing his head to make a sharp turn in my direction.

I smile.

This was my one way of punishing him.

Another day will come.

I've worked up an appetite—an appetite of love.

Luca says he is disappointed he didn't make his gourmet meal. But he throws a beautiful charcuterie board with a special red wine he had saved for a special occasion, and what could be more special than this night? He also promises to make my dinner at another time.

I glance at the time and remind him, "I work for a company where I must be on my toes, and I have to go in early to do some training. Why didn't you drive to pick me up?"

"The whole point of the date night was to walk my date home," he taunts.

"We didn't end up eating, though."

"Don't worry about that. I filled up nicely,"

"Hopefully, the snack will hold you till your next meal. I'm optimistic you won't collapse when you get off all this serotonin."

While in the car, I yawn from exhaustion. That hot sex wore me out! We are both unusually quiet, but Luca's hand is busy with my thighs.

I'm beginning to think he can't get enough.

I pick up my phone after having tossed it aside for over six hours. There are several messages, but thankfully, no calls.

I scroll through, but none look pressing enough to attend to. I am about to put it away when a new notification pops up.

It's Matheo.

Shit, I forgot he existed.

I grit my teeth and swipe open the text.

Hello beautiful,

I'm looking forward to seeing that champagne dress wrapped around your divine body and maybe taking it off, too.

51

I smile lightly and look up, only to be faced with a billboard of Matheo's bar.

To distract myself, I begin to talk about work—any and everything. I point at the billboard, and Luca suddenly presses the brake.

"What!? You work at LE INFINITO?"

"Yes, why?"

"This is hilarious," he lets out a dry chuckle. "Matheo's my dad."

I freeze.

Chapter 7: Afternoon Delight

"Girl!!! Look what the cat drug in?" Connie bellows as soon as the front door swings open.

Somehow, I thought they would have been in bed by now. But thinking of it better, we always wait up for each other unless we were pre-informed that someone wouldn't be showing up that night.

"Add the time! Way past midnight!" Beth chimes in.

I roll my eyes. Ok, Mom.

"OK, now you have to tell us. Were you with your boss?" Connie exclaims, her eyes widening as she kneels on the couch and faces me.

"Wait, what!? Have I been living under a rock? Do you mean Matheo?"

We both ignore Beth's questions, realizing we need to bring her up to speed on the happenings of my life.

"Hailey, come on and share; Beth and I have revealed some deeply personal and intimate details of our lives. For God's sake, I told you about fucking Henry wanting me to engage in a threesome for his sexual gratification."

I finally let out a soft chuckle because Connie was dead serious. By this time, she is up on her feet.

"Yes, Henry was a freak. Has he bothered you anymore?"

Connie answers, "No, but I'm sure he's conspiring something. I ran into a woman he dated before me, and she reassured me I did the right thing, escaping from his web of abuse. After all, he had been on all the dating sites for years and been with countless women. He struggles with the strong, independent type.

Enough about me. What is going on, Hailey?" Connie asks with interest.

"Is that why you've been offering us half-hearted smiles since you walked in?" Connie's countenance changes to that of concern.

"Come here," she adds as she sits on the couch by Beth.

"What's up, Hailey?"

I sigh.

The thought of it is driving me crazy, increasing my mental exhaustion. I try to think of where to start, but no corner seems plausible enough, so I go on.

"Luca is Matheo's son."

As soon as that announcement leaves my mouth, my hands cover my head in frustration.

How did I get here?

"Wait, what!?"

Connie is always the very expressive one. And sometimes overly dramatic, but this time it is needed.

I nod, not knowing what further explanation to provide.

"You mean Matheo, your boss, and Luca, your ex, and you happen to both be seeing both father and son?"

"Touché," I groan.

"Oh my god! How did you find out?"

"Luca said it, when we drove past the bar's sign at the city center."

"Damnnnnnnn…" Beth drags her exclamation in that manner.

"And what did you say?"

"Nothing. I froze. I swallowed saliva. I don't know. I did everything else but speak.

"And he didn't find that weird or suspicious?"

54

"I don't know, Con. I'm exhausted. I don't know what to do," I groan.

"Well, that's easy—" she starts, and I turn to her with a surprised but anticipatory expression. "—date both men till you're sure of how you feel or who you want to be with."

"What!?" Beth and I roar out suddenly.

"That's the most insane thing I've ever heard," I scoff. "Date, father and son!" I exclaim upon realizing that Connie had just said that out loud. "You have been around Henry too long."

"Don't be too opposed to the idea yet. Wait, hear me out."

Connie goes on to explain how she arrived at that thought process.

"You like both of them, Hailey. Or you're attracted to both. It's evident in the things you say, how you speak about them, how you act, everything. It's not normal to see you like that. Forcing your head or body to decide right now is unfair. You don't even know what you're deciding on, the merits, the factors, all of that. So why don't you give yourself time to experience both and be sure of who it would be or if none, rather than making any rash decisions you end up beating yourself up about? Also, we can't decide if that's where you will go. Allow yourself to experience this affection and watch how you react to both. You'll make better choices that way."

"And if it continues to be both?"

"It wouldn't be both, trust me--or you walk away from both at the end of the day."

My eyes widen. The latter part isn't something I will be looking forward to.

Connie sounds like she already had the answer to who he would prefer me with in mind but would rather not say it, probably for fear of it being the wrong choice.

"You know what, I think I agree," Beth finally chips in after brooding.

She nods repeatedly and adds her two cents to crown all of Connie's explanation.

"I honestly think this would be a bad idea. Two incredible men cut from the same cloth and have the same blood flowing through them. They would most likely woo me similarly and with the same intensity. Plus, for how long can I keep this up? I just told Luca where I worked tonight. What if he figures it out?"

I shake my head frantically. "I don't know, I don't know, I don't know."

"The answer will find you soon, Hailey. Relax," Connie assures.

"Speaking of Luca. You mentioned being with him, and you returned super late. Is there something we should know?" Beth asks.

My cheeks heat up instantly. "I don't kiss and tell, but let's just say it was an exciting evening."

"Woahhhhh!" Connie is yelling and tugging closer to me.

We eventually hit the hay, and then in the morning, the doorbell rings,

"It's too early," Beth mouths before getting up to check who it is.

"A delivery guy," she whispers again. "With a huge box too."

"Leave it there, thank you!"

"Oh no. I need Miss Hailey to sign, please."

Beth yells for me to answer it.

I sign, take the box in, and place it on our center table. Everyone is eager to see the content, especially who it's from.

Beth had already hinted that this was one point in favor of the sender as I opened up the package and lifted the note.

"Omg!" I get up in shock.

"What!!?"

56

"Read it to us!"

Miss Hailey,

Come this weekend, the most extensive art exhibition will be happening in Italy. Hailey, I have been invited as a special guest, and it would be my absolute delight if you could free up your schedule and be my plus one.

Do not worry about expenses, as I will wine and dine you.

If it's a yes, I can't wait to see you, especially in that dress.

I am looking forward to hearing from you.

Yours majestically,

Matheo.

"Pick up your phone now and send that answer!" Connie squeals.

"What!? And what about Luca?"

"What about him? You want to pass up on a trip to Italy to see what you love most because of your ex?" she scoffs.

I chuckle. These girls can't be serious. They make me do the most unimaginable things.

It was not like I would turn down the offer anyway; they should at least allow me to feel guilty for desiring the trip.

Instantly, I pick up my phone and place a call to Matheo. But on second thought, I end it and send a text instead.

All the while, Beth holds out the gold sequin dress with a low back, and her mouth remains agape.

The gold strap heels, and the delectable clutch purse fit perfectly like a pair.

It is beyond stunning. Words cannot describe it.

I restrain myself from rushing off to fit into it, but I can already tell how perfectly it would hug my curves and show my toned back.

Anticipation fills me.

They grumble for me to try it on.

It fits like a glove.

*****

The following Sunday afternoon, Luca comes to pick me up around four.

We had texted several times before he sent me an Instagram post of a music festival he would love us to attend.

Of course, I accepted wholeheartedly, looking forward to all the time I can spend with him.

And the toe-curling sex that would follow.

I bite my lip at the intrusive thought when my doorbell rings, and I know it's him.

Luca smiles as I open the door and kisses me sweetly and gently.

I would drag him to my bedroom if the roommates weren't here.

We arrive at Riverside Park and notice the scenic view of the Hudson River and the New Jersey shoreline. My eyes widen at how much activity is happening, and I am suddenly more eager than I was minutes ago. We can hear a reggae band in the background.

We start at the entrance and look at the promotional merchandise, and we both get a Red Hot Chili Peppers t-shirt, for they are the headliners.

We walk by the food and drink stand, grab a couple of beers, and walk further down to the stage where the crowd is gathered.

The festival lasts for three days, and today is the final show. Several bands will be on before the Chili Peppers perform.

It already looks so promising.

While many activities go on, people are dancing as the artists perform, and Luca and I sing along to many of the songs at the top of our lungs each time.

Indeed, this is the most fun I have had in days, and this all seems so right.

Music playing too loud would get on my nerves, which is hilarious, knowing I work in a bar. But that's precisely why. Plus, they play the same songs almost all the time. Seeing and hearing the music live is different than the club stuff.

The energy is all around, transmitting from person to person.

Luca and I take a few breaks to walk around and see other park areas. Finding a private park area leads us to some afternoon delight.

Luca is always looking for angles and stays one step ahead of everyone. In this situation, Luka finds a secluded place, even surprising himself. The mere thought excites me more than the night at his house with the looming fear of being caught. There is nothing like making love with nature and the soft sounds of the music playing softly in the background.

Luca takes hold of my hand, kisses it, and gently guides me to a sweet, soft patch of grass. He gazes at me, puts his hands around my waist, and gently pulls me in for a sweet tongue-lashing. He continues to kiss the entire time except for the attention he gives my nipples.

I am trying to keep my moans at a minimum.

My hand touches his thigh only to discover a hard cock. Our time is very limited, so we get to it. Luca enters me tenderly, and we are facing one another. I am ready; he knows how to hit all the right spots. It is exhilarating and hot as he enters me but tenderly executes. It doesn't take long as we reach climax together. I feel like we are making love and not fucking.

Luca and I adjust our clothing as we are still kissing. We walk out of the overgrown area with smiles.

After we devour a couple of street tacos, we talk nonstop about things that concern us, and I see we are on the same page. And then I hear a voice.

"Luca!?" a feminine voice calls out behind us, and we swirl around.

My smile seizes immediately, and I am curious about the woman who is interrupting our conversation and is walking towards us.

"Hey, Miller, how are you doing?" he greets her somewhat excitedly, and they go in for a hug.

My chest tightens.

Who is this woman? I scream internally.

They begin talking, but it doesn't take a minute for Luca to notice I'm not behind him, so he pulls me closer and holds on.

That's cute.

He introduces her as his ex and me as his woman, and I am shocked by that but find it very acceptable. My jealousy doesn't even have time to marinate as he holds me in place and plants kisses on my forehead and lips as he speaks to Miller.

I love the touch. I love that Luca indirectly lets her know he cares for me.

I love the assurance he is subtly providing me with.

I love h—

Hailey!

I straighten myself out, and we finally walk away. There's no point discussing anything, as he has already shown good intentions with me.

I blush lightly.

"Luca, I should tell you something," I stop abruptly.

"Okay?"

"I'll be traveling next week—on a business trip."

"Okay? Is that it? You'll be coming back, right?"

"Yes," I burst out laughing. "Definitely."

"Oh, good. I was already thinking about the things I would pack with the new life I would be running away with you to start. We can live off a diet of laughter, mischief, and good sex."

He was too cute.

Another beautiful night with Luca.

He was too cute.

He can't find out who I will be going with. Also, I will refrain, or at least do my best.

Chapter 8: Italy

It's Wednesday, and I'm starting to get cold feet. Our flight leaves tomorrow morning, and I still have time to back out, but this is an opportunity I can't pass up. Indeed, I can keep Matheo's hands off me.

There was a time when I felt differently.

I breeze through work that day absentmindedly, trying to focus primarily on what to expect during the trip.

At some points, I feel like I made a hasty decision without properly thinking things through.

How do I behave around Matheo? Would we stay in the same bed? Would I have to sleep with him? PDAs, all of that?

My subconscious is going at me furiously, and I'm losing my mind. I don't know what I thought would happen after accepting such an offer—an all-expense paid trip to Italy.

The uncertainty is unsettling, so after checking in with Hulio, and Jenna saying she can take my shift I take off work earlier than usual.

I arrive home, and the girls are already back. It's surprising, but I do not ask questions as I'm also not in the mood.

"Clearly, someone's not going to miss us," Beth roars, pushing my bedroom door open.

"You know that's impossible," I state while she and Connie enter.

"So what's going on?"

"I'm afraid, guys. I'm not sure of what I'm getting into."

"I'm traveling with a man I hardly know. I know the trip will be exciting and adventurous, but knowing our history, I think he will want more than companionship. I need to find the strength to trust my instincts and make the right decision.

Connie gives me a soft pat on the back and says, "You're going to see the most exquisite art display in the world, and the Italian food and culture are yours for the taking. Also, you mentioned you've had some captivating conversations with Matheo."

But no matter how far, we're here for you," Connie leans closer and assures.

"We'll be by the phone 24/7," Beth adds, waving her phone in my face."

Yes, and I'll be on the other side of the world.

"Girl, if you keep up this energy, you will have a bad trip. So, let loose right now! We're with you.

"Okay, if you must know, I made arrangements with Andy to be on speed dial if you need help or must escape. Hopefully, it won't come to that. So make sure you leave your live location on at all times and keep us posted on your well-being. Sound Good?"

Andy was Beth's ex. Yeah, best ex-boyfriend. They ended on the best terms because his parents recalled him back to Italy after school with a whole new life waiting for him. They may end up together since Beth hasn't been with anyone else after him, but who knows?

"You guys are the best!"

"We know," Beth says shyly, and we go in for a hug.

Honestly, what would I do without these girls?

*****

Matheo and I land in Milan at almost midnight after a nine-hour flight.

We are exhausted on arrival and waste no time checking into our room.

Yes, we are sharing a room.

We had slept through most of the flight, and he mentioned a few times that he couldn't wait to rest on a bed; I certainly could relate. But was I in that equation?

The room is like stepping into a world of elegance and class. Matheo orders room service, and the freshly prepared pasta is a true feast for the senses. I can't help but savor every bite. Of course, I think of Luca and his culinary skills. I'll bet he could wing this dish.

I moan several times with each bite and see Matheo steal glances at me.

I am sure I do not want to give Matheo any ideas, so I immediately put myself together. I send my girls a picture of the before and after of my plate and rave about how delightful the meal was.

After a few minutes, I get in bed while Matheo remains on the collapsible couch in the living room area. The silence between us has been unusually awkward, and I know I can attribute it to the level of stress and jet lag, but I am hoping my anxiety isn't evident.

Matheo wakes me up the next day, and I have little to no memories of when I dozed off. I look to the other side of the bed, and it appears unused.

I have no idea what to think, so I turn to him and offer my morning pleasantries.

"Afternoon, sunshine," he laughed. "I kept hoping you would wake up, but you looked so peaceful. You looked pretty beautiful while you were sleeping, might I add."

I can't believe how long I slept. My eyes widen at the realization that it is getting late and I'm in Italy and wasting the day away, so

I jump out of bed. Matheo is wearing a tailored Italian suit with suspenders over his shoulders.

I apologize for sleeping so long. Matheo didn't seem to care; he brushes it off and says, "We're still on time as long as you don't spend all day in the bathroom."

I gulp down some coffee and hasten my step.

I come out in forty minutes, literally dressed like a Barbie doll. I take my bath in ten minutes, fit into my dress in another ten, and do my makeup and hair in record-breaking time.

I am impressed with the reflection I see in the mirror.

Like I presumed, the sequin dress hugs my curves a little too perfectly. The low drape at the back falls just above my butt crack, leaving my entire back in view. I am happy I took Connie's suggestion to pick up a piece of gold jewelry because it makes me ten times hotter.

My makeup is primarily nude but bronzy to give my face the same shine my entire look has. My hair is elegantly pinned up and loose, allowing a few curls to cascade over my shoulders.

"Damn," Matheo mutters after a few minutes of gaping at me.

I feel my cheeks flush red in excitement. I'm glad Matheo approves, but my second self worries about his intentions.

As he walks closer to me, he kisses my hand, then my forehead, before complimenting me.

Honestly, he is too sweet.

He offers to help me finish accessorizing and gets on his knees to assist me in strapping my heels. As he's securing the shoes, his fingers gently brush against my leg, sending a subtle shiver down my spine, and I freeze.

For a second, anyway.

I was caught in the allure of his hand touching me as his hand made its way to my inner thigh. I would call this seduction to the highest degree. He stroked my skin, reaching around the back of my leg, inching up to my ass where he could grab a cheek. He was about to lift the entire dress as he moved his other hand to snatch the other cheek when there was a knock on the door.

"Sir, Mr. Ricci, Your car is waiting!"

Being startled, I pull away and get my bearings about myself. Matheo sighs, and he apologizes for getting carried away.

"Are you okay? I couldn't help myself, Hailey. You look so beautiful, and those legs, that ass."

He tells me it is more than an attraction; he enjoys my company.

I reassure him, "I'm okay and glad we hit the brakes on this."

I remind him I would like to know him better, and my mind is elsewhere. After all, we are in Italy.

Up until now he has been quite the gentleman. His magnetic presence and undeniable charm are sexy. His appeal and allure are indeed heart-melting, for he has the uncanny ability to captivate and turn on women.

I can't stop thinking about Luca. What am I doing?

We are on our way to Plaza Borromeo on Lake Maggiore. Taking the ferry from Stresa is
the most convenient way to get there, but also the only way to reach many of these enchanting destinations. The ferry ride is full of captivating views of the Italian countryside.

It's a few minutes past five when we arrive at Palazzo Borromeo on Lake Maggiore. Matheo and I are welcomed by a charming square adorned with elegant buildings and picturesque gardens. The exterior is majestic, and I exclaim in awe—such a historical treasure and a cultural hub.

I have only seen pictures in magazines or on the internet and dreamed of being here. Finally, seeing it is beyond what words can describe. All those who write about it undermine the heavenly aura the place holds.

Matheo takes my hand in his, and we walk in together, grabbing a glass of Prosecco the servers held at the entrance. The event has already begun, so we waste no time gracing them with our presence.

The program of events merely lasts over an hour to mark the anniversary of the gallery and allow guests to feed their eyes with new additions.

I stroll over to the balcony overlooking the lake, and I have never seen a large body of water look so enticing. A hand goes around my waist, brushing the visible parts of my skin, and goosebumps engulf me. I turn around to see Matheo, and my body relaxes.

Why am I relaxed around him?

"I have somewhere else to show you."

I am intrigued, and I follow him immediately without any questions.

We visit the Gallery of General Berthier privately, and my mouth drops open. The gallery houses a collection of over 130 paintings and extraordinary pieces not available to the general public.

It's like seeing the coming of Christ. With watery eyes, I turn around and mouth a "thank you" to Matheo before walking further to examine them closely.

Everything is so beautiful, and the history of it all is fascinating, and I perfectly enunciate that with each gasp I let out as I proceed.

Art is indeed life.

I glance over my shoulders and see Matheo observing me, hand in his pocket, with a look of satisfaction. I can't deny that he earned it because I was pretty fucking happy.

Matheo and I converse about the paintings I've seen online and what I read about them, and I tell him what I think of them. I give him my depictions of the art and sometimes ask him to pitch in. Matheo engages me.

After what feels like an eternity, we exit that space and visit the other rooms within the "place of delights," as it's fondly called. We see the Throne room next and the Queen's room shortly after that.

Matheo finally leads me into the garden, and the first thing I notice is how dark the clouds are, so I check the time to see it's already past ten. The lighting of the interior did not give that away.

We admire the beautiful array of LED lights that adorn the gardens. The famous baroque garden with the Teatro Massimo at the center has ten terraces shaped like a truncated pyramid.

I am in awe of Count Vitaliano Borromeo and the history he bestowed on Milan.

Everything is a sight to behold: the monumental unicorn, the obelisks, the statues, the two towers, all the mighty trees and every other architectural element.

"Ready to call it a night?"

"I mean, I don't have much of a choice. This place is beyond amazing, Matheo. Thank you for giving me this chance."

"Anything for you, beautiful."

"Stop by and have dinner?"

Maybe the dinner will slow him down.

We decide to go to our hotel restaurant, Il Baretto al Baglioni. They will be closing soon, so we don't have the luxury of going through the menu. Matheo, however, promises that we will return.

We enjoy course after course, and the food atmosphere is a turn-on. While we eat we share a rare bottle of Chianti Classico.

At every point in time during the evening Matheo had whipped out his phone, taking the most amazing pictures of me—in each corner of the gallery and at the restaurant, so I look through them while we finish our wine. I also thank Matheo for such a wonderful day and evening. Everything I experienced was pure joy.

Just hoping he's tired. He was quite capable of seducing me. I have to control myself!

"Matheo?" I announce as soon as we settle in our room.

"Yeah?"

"Can I ask you a question?"

"Why not?"

"You never talk about your family. Wife? Kids? None of that."

He lets out a low grumble, and I'm unsure if I have touched the wrong subject.

"If you can't answer it, it's alright. I'm sorry if I—"

"Don't apologize for seeking clarity, Princess. And it's alright," he interjects and clears his throat. "My wife died a few years ago and I have just one child, a son, but unfortunately, we are estranged."

"Oh, oh my goodness. I'm so sorry.

"Hailey..." this time around, it comes out like a warning, "...there's nothing to be sorry for."

So sad. I nod my head, and he changes the subject.

"What do you think about owning an art gallery?"

Now he's seducing me.

"It's an amazing dream. I once nurtured it, maybe I still do, but for now—"

"I think I asked the wrong question. How would you feel if you were allowed to own a gallery right now?"

"What!?" I exclaim.

"Matheo, I'm flattered that you want me to have my dreams, but I could never accept such a gift. That's a giant ticket to fill. It sounds crazy, but I'll have to think about it."

I guess I do have some moral standards.

"Alright, as you wish, Hailey, it is your world. Get some rest, pretty face. We have a tour to wake up tomorrow or later today," he corrects himself, as it is well past twelve.

*****

I wake up to see Matheo studying my face. I smile and stretch, and he brings me coffee in bed. It would be so easy to fall for him.

Maybe I am.

Matheo's limousine arrives while I'm in the dressing room, so he calls out to me.

I step out, and once again, he showers me with compliments despite being dressed rather casually in denim jeans and a ribbed crop top. I wear my favorite walking sandals and join him outside the door.

The tour of the city is more than I expected. We see a lot of fascinating structures with history to go with. We stop by the magnificent Milan Cathedral known as Duomo. The sheer grandeur of its Gothic architecture leaves one in awe. We climb to the rooftop, admiring Milan's panoramic view, showcasing the city's mix of ancient and contemporary structures.

We stop at a famous cafe to have an espresso, try my first cannoli, and buy souvenirs. There's just so much to see. Matheo thought it cute that I never had a cannoli. I tease him and say, "Haha, you got me. Thanks for inducing me to such a sweet, delicious dessert."

Almost as sweet as him

I can't deny I am having the time of my life. But that little voice in me tells me this is all wrong.

As we enter the limo to tour Milan's artistic streets, Matheo has a bottle of French Champagne open. This isn't very clear to me, and

I ask, "Here we are in Italy; why aren't we drinking Italian Champagne?"

Matheo laughs as he pours and gives me the low down. "My dear, Italy is known for its sparkling wines. True Champagne only comes exclusively from the Champagne region of France. Champagne, France, is an actual place, and in my opinion, there's nothing better than French Champagne. However, Italy produces exceptional sparkling wines worth exploring, called Prosecco. They were serving it at the art gallery.

I was impressed by his knowledge of wine. This man is so exciting and attractive. Maybe I should rethink this situation.

I need to control myself.

Matheo raises his glass and says, "Here's to a beautiful friendship." We clink glasses and sip the Champagne, causing me to feel an explosion of bubbles tickling my tongue. Matheo and I continue to drink the bottle, and then he opens another. At this point, we are laughing and having a good with casual flirting when Matheo gets very close to me. At this point, I'm drunk, and my inhibitions are compromised.

Really drunk.

Amidst Champagne's bubbling laughter, I find myself in a situation. Is it the Champagne, or am I drawn to him?

Matheo's undeniable magnetism captivates me with a longing gaze and the soft touch of his lips as he gently took hold of my hair and tugged at it, pulling me closer. The kiss intensifies as he nibbles on my bottom lip, and our tongues were in perfect harmony. His hands in my hair are now heading toward my breast, and his body draws closer, pressing me to lie on my back. I can see his cock is hard. His kisses move toward my neck, and he lifts my shirt. He enjoys my breasts momentarily but doesn't waste too much time there before he slips off my jeans. His tongue trickles down my

71

belly, and he is about to pull my panties off. When I look into his hungry eyes, guilt washes over me.

Eyes like Luca's, yes, dumbass, that's his dad.

I sit up abruptly, creating distance between us, his hands still on my body.

"Are you alright?" Matheo gasps out, his hands still on my body.

"Yeah," I lie and nod, but uncertainty is visible on my face.

He looks at me with concern, and I begin apologizing. For what? I have no idea.

"Hey, relax. We'll soon head back so you can rest."

He kisses me again, not as passionately as before, but somehow, he is not caring that I have reservations.

Just as his hands reach the clasp of my bra, I yell out, "Matheo, stop!"

He winces and moves back immediately.

I feel utterly terrible, with overwhelming guilt, remorse, and self-blame.

"I'm in love with someone else," I blurt out.

In love? I have no idea how those words flew out of my mouth, but I knew they were true.

I see the shock in his expression and a slight glimpse of anger. I don't want to see that. I don't want to be in that car with him. I want fresh air. I want space.

I want Luca.

With tears in my eyes, I dress quickly and ask the driver to pull over. My hands wander around till they find the door handle. Still facing him, I pull it open and climb out, but not before mouthing an apology, "Matheo, I'm sorry."

I return to our hotel room and pack up my suitcase. As I'm leaving the lobby, I see a glimpse of Matheo sitting at the bar, and he's not alone. He's with a beautiful blond having a martini. He certainly didn't look upset to me.

He's already over me, which should have bothered me.

I couldn't care less.

I grab a cab for the airport in time for the last flight headed back to New York.

Nine hours later, I land, and the first place my legs take me to is Luca's home.

Should I leave it alone or tell him the truth?

Luca is surprised to see me. He kisses me sweetly, and it is apparent he did miss me.

"Aren't you supposed to be back tomorrow?"

"I'm just going to say it. I love you, Luca. I want to be with you."

The astonishment on his face keeps him from saying anything, but the eagerness with which he jumps to my lips gives me all the answers I need.

Chapter 9: Breakfast in Bed

I wake up the following day to the ray of morning sun that pierces through the window. I have a deep sense of emotional closeness to Luca. He cherishes, desires, and appreciates me. He is my guy.

But Luca is nowhere to be found.

I toss around for a while before I finally sit up and notice a small note by the side of the bed. And a glass of water.

"Drink this. I'll be in the kitchen prepping your breakfast."

I smile.

After wearing ourselves out all night, he still gets up early to make me breakfast.

I climb out of bed and get into the bathroom to wash my mouth and go out to meet him, but before I can finish, Luca already waltzes into the room, singing at the top of his lungs.

I laugh and make myself visible from the bathroom to see a tray in his hand with the most colorful array of breakfast.

"I do need to get my strength back from my workout last night," as I dig into the vegetable frittata, whole wheat buttered toast, fresh fruit, fresh squeezed orange juice, and the best strong black coffee.

I chuckle in delight. "Did you do all of this?"

"Yes, since the cook was off today, silly, I did."

I am impressed.

"What do you take me for?" he whines.

Luca is on me in seconds, showering my face and upper body with kisses.

We play like lovers for a minute before he suggests I finish my breakfast before it gets cold.

I could get used to this.

I ask him to join me, so he snuggles over, and I set the tray in our midst. While we eat, he asks me to tell him about my trip, and I nearly choke on the last bite of toast.

I do well with my narration, leaving out the essential part I am not ready for him to be made aware of despite the fact I am now confident I want nothing to do with Matheo.

I am terrified of how badly he will take the news.

Just then, there's a repeated click on his alarm system, and he grumbles before getting up and staggering to the door.

"Stay put, I'll be right back!" Luca enjoins as he walks out of sight.

I fill my mouth with food and try to block out the intrusive thoughts that want to ruin the perfect morning.

I haven't checked my phone and haven't seen it since I arrived here, so I look around for it. I know the girls would have bombarded me with calls and messages on seeing my live location. They have to know I'm back by now. I search further as it's nowhere around me when I hear the yells from Luca's living room.

"Why are you both here? What is this? Some form of ambush?" he bellows, and I can tell he's pacing back and forth.

"It's nothing like that. You need to calm down and listen to what we have to say," the first voice admonishes.

"Luca, sit down, please. We are trying to tell you something significant," the second pleads.

I hear the living room quiet, and I assume they are shuffling to find seats.

I mind my business since the tension in the air has dissipated when I hear the first two words that drop out of the visitor's mouth.

"Your father would kill us if he knew we were here or the ones that gave him up. The club is yours," the bombshell drops.

My eyes go wide.

"What!?" I hear Luca's shock.

"Your mother built it from the ground up, and when she knew she was going to pass away, willed it to you to take over as soon as you finished school."

"We met your father often when we heard you were out of school to follow through on your mother's wishes. Sometimes, he dismissed us with promises to do so. Other times, it was an outright ousting."

I couldn't see, but I can imagine how frantic Luca must be. The silence in that room is deafening. Even I am livid.

The conversation between the men ends. Luca thanks them and ushers them out, reassuring them he would be in touch.

I almost run back to bed before I realize it's a bad idea, and Luca may need comfort now.

"What kind of father would do that to their son? Would he lie through his teeth and care less about the things that concern his son?

Actually, both my parent would have stabbed me in the back, especially for money.

After hearing all this, I knew Matheo had fooled me. He wasn't the man I thought he was!" Lucas continues to rant as soon as I come into plain sight.

His eyes are bloodshot, and the stress on his face is strong enough to form blades with his tightened jaw.

I want to tell him about Matheo and me so bad now, with thoughts that he would feel all his anger and hate all at once and get over it.

But what kind of sinister thing to do is that? After finding out his dad is actively swindling him from his inheritance, he is vulnerable.

I don't think now is the time to tell him about Matheo.

I am profoundly conflicted, so I refrain from doing something I may regret.

I go over to hold Luca and comfort him.

"I'm sorry, Luca. I can't pretend to understand how betrayed you feel, but I want you to know I'll be here to hold and support you every step of the way. I'm here to listen, and you'll never be alone in this situation."

"It's okay, baby. I'll deal with my dad later. For now, I should get you to your besties. They've been blowing up your phone," as he comes to me and holds me tight.

I should be comforting him; instead, he makes me feel safe and secure.

*****

"Girl, where have you been?"

"You are in the States, and you didn't come home. Where did you go?"

"I'll get to that later."

I hear an all too familiar voice, and my heart thumps faster against my chest. I push past my girls to see Matheo sitting comfortably on the couch in our living room like he belonged there.

They grin at me, but I'm sending death stares back and acting like I've gone all insane, trying to ask them why he was in our house and what they have done.

"Shit!" Connie mutters, and I can tell she has seen why I'm fretting as Luca is on the phone outside talking with his lawyers about the club.

Connie and Beth push past me, and I'm sure it's to stall Luca.

Please don't let him walk in on this.

"Why are you here!?" I affirm sternly but deep down, beyond terrified.

"Well, someone ran off in the middle of our trip, got to the hotel room to find all your things gone, and my curiosity piqued. Why did you have such an outburst?" Matheo stops as though pondering the question he didn't want an answer to, and I also provide none.

"I had you investigated, and lo and behold, here is why?"

"You what!? Are you out of your mind? I yell. I'm not your property."

By this time, I am irritated. Matheo believes he can snoop around my life like that. He's presenting me with pictures of Luca and me, but I pay no attention to that as he has just intruded on my life in more ways than many.

"What's going on here—Dad!???"

"Oh shit!" I mumble under my breath.

The girls have done a terrible job of keeping him away.

"What the fuck is going on here!? Hailey?"

I couldn't.

"Well, I'll help you. I was in Italy with my girlfriend here."

"Your what!?"

"I'm not your girlfriend!" Luca and I burst out at the same time.

How can I ever recover from this?

78

I look to Luca to plead with my eyes to explain with my faltering words, but the disappointment, pain, anger, and resentment that all cross his face simultaneously are evident.

"Luca, I can explain. It's not what it looks like. I didn't betray you. It was supposed to be a work trip like I told you when he came on to me."

"Please!" Luca raises his hand and shuts up my rambling. "You both deserve each other," he hisses at me, and that cut through me. I could feel the piercing pain in my chest.

My eyes water as I look at Luca, but he tears his gaze away and focuses on Matheo.

I could see the resentment boiling in Luca's face.

"Father, I'm on to you now, and I always have been. You ruined much of my childhood and took me away from Hailey. Now you're back trying to take her away again. Who knows what lengths you have gone to, and I can only imagine how you manipulated her with your wealth and lost promises.

I saw what you did to my mother with your infidelity and how you skillfully made her feel it was her fault. I watched her slowly die while you were galvanizing around chasing women. You had no regard for her or me. And to think I was contemplating mending our relationship. Have at it with Hailey," and his gaze pierces through me.

"I once thought she was my everything; I was wrong. Also, Dad, I know about LE INFINITO; it is mine! You will hear from my lawyers sooner than you think."

He slams the door, and Matheo follows him out as he also gives me an unpleasant stare.

I fall to my knees and weep.

Chapter 10: Forever

I spend the next month with an overwhelming feeling of grief and loss. The sadness and sorrow empty my soul, imagining my life without Luca. Connie and Beth are regretful for encouraging me to go with Matheo to Italy. The hopelessness and uncertainty about the future put a spear through my heart.

Fear and anxiety of being able to love again. I will always love Luca.

And I think that is even more painful.

My girls regularly check on me, pity evident on their faces. I'm not too fond of their reaction, but I feel pity for myself, too.

How did I go from having the best of both worlds to nothing?

It's called selfishness, Hailey.

And I said it from the start: I didn't want to take more than I could give. I didn't want to lead anyone on, let alone father and son. I knew I couldn't handle it. I asked for help in making this decision. And that's what it was, my decision.

I tried contacting Luca shortly after that, but he reiterated that he didn't want to see me. I decided to give him space. And I ask myself if I have left him enough room each time. When is the best time to reach out again?

Days after that, too, I quit the bar. Since Matheo was the owner, returning to work was out of the question. The environment would be toxic for me, and the chances of being fired are even higher. I didn't want that kind of drama in my life. There was no way I could handle seeing Matheo after all that.

My life has become a rollercoaster of destructive emotions. I swing from anger to annoyance to hurt to pity, depression, you name it. I can count the number of times I smiled or laughed, and it wasn't many.

I am not too fond of the way I had let someone ruin my own love life. Although, as much as I didn't want to admit it, I was thoroughly responsible.

Again.

Finally, today, I decide to say goodbye to my horizontal position and leave my bed to live my life again.

It is going to take me a long while to feel better, and I am sure I will still reach out to Luca at least one more time. But for that moment, I know I can't continue to wallow in self-pity.

I've never been much religious, but today, I'm on my knees, praying Luca will someday forgive me.

And love me again.

I have made a mess now. I need to clean it up or forget.

I choose the latter.

I begin to meditate and do breathwork daily. I also am painting again. I create one masterpiece after another. Connie and Beth are impressed with my work and happy to see me return to life. I sell a few on eBay to pay the bills and get a handsome amount for them. The paintings are a variety of abstract birds; mainly, I painted the bluebird, as I would call it, the bird of happiness.

Wishful fucking thinking.

After hours of trying to imitate the hotel pasta I had in Italy, I realize I should stick to painting. I settle in front of the TV. I am flicking through channels when I hear Luca's name.

I call the girls.

He had taken his father to court over ownership of the bar, and the press was there live, waiting on the final verdict.

81

It's surprising that I never saw the similarities in surnames, the same eyes or knew how wealthy they were before being entangled with them.

I tune in late, so it's already over as I see Luca and his team of lawyers walking out first, victory spread across their faces.

Luca addresses one reporter, and he confirms the victory.

I smile painfully.

I'm excited for him but not too fond of the memory I left him with.

I pick up my phone and send a congratulatory text alongside another apology for how things ended with us, and I see him glance at it on TV.

If he doesn't reach out to me anymore, I'll take comfort in seeing a slight smile on his face as soon as my message is delivered.

I go about the rest of my day trying to do anything to distract myself. Luca, I understand that reading my text and not getting any response is killing me.

The girls are trying to indulge me in exciting activities and are happy that I stepped out of my room that day.

I consider going to bed early; that weak, sad feeling is in my heart again. I'm sure if I could shed another tear, but it is bound to happen just as sure as my heart will still beat.

Ding dong.

"Expecting someone?" Connie asks me.

"Not at all."

We all look at each other before Beth heads for the door. Beth has her Spotify on and

Sacrifice by Elton John is playing:

> And it's no sacrifice
> Just a simple word.
> It's two hearts living

In two separate worlds.

And there he is, Luca, a bouquet in hand.

My eyes water up immediately, and I run to him. I sob my apologies and explanations into his chest while he holds me tight. He said he would have come for me all the while but needed to get the four cases out of the way and keep me away from his fight with his dad. Adding he needed the time to process all of this.

"I wanted to be sure, Hailey." I take Luca to our deck, so we have some privacy.

"I love you, Hailey. I always have, I always will. At my beginning, middle, and end. Hailey, I promise to love you forever. I cherish every moment and know I'm ready to invest my every effort into rebuilding what we once had. The pain of our separation has awakened the depth of my love for you."

I feel like I am alive again, the blood running through my body. I have a pulse again.

Luca and I go to his house that evening, and we sit down and have a heart-to-heart. I explain I only had been with Matheo several times but never fucked him. I am honest and tell him I did consider it, and my notion changed when he surfaced into my life again. Matheo's wealth and power were seductive but not enough. A love like ours was hard to find.

Truth has a way of revealing itself, even if it takes time.

*****

Luca can't stop talking about the bar and how his mother started it all from scratch while still alive. As a young boy, he had always wanted to take over the bar someday and get it to greater heights. He shares his plans with me; they are so phenomenal I couldn't help but agree with him.

I am so excited and grateful to share this moment with him. I can't believe I ever doubted my love for him and how he made me feel. The days away from him were torture, and I never want to return to that.

Luca has made me realize time and time again that love is real. It's just as real as air and feels even better when you're loved right back. I look around the room and notice something different. There on the wall is one of my paintings I sold on eBay. It was my favorite and his as well.

I'm in his arms again, and I'm never leaving.

After we make mad, passionate love, I sigh with ultimate satisfaction. I couldn't be happier when he asks me to move in.

I manage to reply with a smile and a kiss, "Of course."

Luca offers me a spot at the bar—the same offer Matheo proposed.

With no strings attached.

I work at the bar and have my art section in the wine-tasting room, which Luca and I added after he took over. It opened up a new world of audiences, connections, and opportunities. Excited about the plan, he suggested we put some original paintings into print. And only print a limited amount of them. We could retail them along with the wine. Our minds were coming together in business and love. What more could anyone ask for?

I start getting calls and many more orders with our online store.

"Hailey, we are selling almost as much art as wine. Customers are going crazy for it."

I giggle, holding onto his hand. "Of course they are. You're a genius, and you're good at this."

"Is that a compliment I hear?" Luca asks, winking at me.

Before I can reply, though, we stop as we almost bump into Matheo. My eyes go wide, and the hairs on my skin stand. I'm not scared, just surprised. I haven't seen him since the last time. It's been a while.

Matheo's eyes slowly move from Luca to me and back to Luca. His expression is blank, and I can't tell what he is thinking. "You're back with her?"

Luca's hands hold mine tighter as if trying to reassure me that he is here and won't let anything happen. "Yes, as you can see."

"Why?" Matheo asks, and I bite the insides of my cheeks. I don't hate him. I wish things would have been different. I wish I hadn't met him the way I had. I wish I met him as Luca's father so I could have strived for his approval. He is the father of the man I love, after all.

Luca glares. "Because I love her and would spend the rest of my life with her."

My eyes snap at Matheo and wonder, would he spend the rest of his life with me?

For ten minutes Matheo looks between us again, and to our surprise, he smiles. "Well then, can you handle the bar? With great power comes great responsibility."

Luca completes, "I know the saying, father. With Hailey..." he raises my hand to his lips and kisses the back of my palm. "...I can."

Matheo nods. "Good luck, son. She's a good one."

He smiles at me and walks away. I have to pinch myself to make sure I am not dreaming.

Just when I thought Matheo was gone, he stops, turns, and gestures for Luca to walk over.

Matheo tells Luca, "Son, reflecting on my journey as a father, I realize I should have been better. I know I was wrong with your Mother, and I have shame about it. I hide behind these beautiful younger women, which feels suitable for the moment. But in all reality, I know deep inside, a woman my age would be better to build a stable life. I want to be a better man and a better father. Maybe someday, a grandfather? Could you consider starting over? What I'm asking is, will you ever forgive me."

Luca and Matheo, both on the verge of tears, hug each other. I am taken aback but am also overwhelmed with joy for both. Luca dries his eyes and says his goodbyes to his dad. They make plans to talk later in the week.

He has a smile on his face as he returns and hugs me while he's shaking with utter joy.

Luca declares, "I forgave him. We are taking baby steps, but it's a start; he is my dad."

Family.

As I squeeze the shit out of his hand, we stop and look at each other.

"What?" Luca asks.

I shrug. "You're going to spend the rest of your life with me?"

He smiles, and I see those sincere green eyes. "I will. If you let me."

I smile and nod. "I love you, Luca."

"And I love you, Hailey."

About the Author

EVA LUCAS is an up-and-coming writer and was born and raised in Southern Illinois. Eva draws inspiration from the diverse experiences she has encountered being poised to make a significant impact with her heartfelt and soul-stirring stories that leave a lasting impression on all who read them.

Made in the USA
Monee, IL
21 October 2023

44948181R00049